-HAUNTED HISTORY-

THE *QUEEN MARY* IS HAUNTED!

MARIE MORRISON

PowerKiDS press.

NEW YORK

Published in 2021 by The Rosen Publishing Group, Inc.
29 East 21st Street, New York, NY 10010

First edition

Portions of this work were originally authored by Therese Shea and published as *Haunted! The* Queen Mary. All new material this edition authored by Marie Morrison

Editor: Jill Keppeler
Book Design: Rachel Rising

Photo Credits: Cover, Philip Pilosian/Shutterstock.com; pp. 1-32 (background) Slava Gerj/Shutterstock.com; p. 5 Angel DiBilio/Shutterstock.com; p. 7 Bob Thomas/Popperfoto/Contributor/Getty Images; p. 9 Keystone/Stringer/Hulton Archive/Getty Images; p. 11 Haywood Magee/Stringer/Picture Post/Getty Images; p. 13 Ron Case/Stringer/Hulton Archive/Getty Images; p. 15 GagliardiPhotography/Shutterstock.com; p. 17 Phillip Faraone/Stringer/Getty Images Entertainment/Getty Images; p. 19 Fox Photos/Stringer/Hulton Archive/Getty Images; p. 21 MauhMauh/Shutterstock.com; pp. 23, 25 MediaNews Group/Orange County Register via Getty Images/Contributor/Getty Images; p. 27 FREDERIC J. BROWN/Staff/AFP/Getty Images; p. 28 HECTOR MATA/Staff/AFP/Getty Images; p. 29 AnjelikaGr/Shuttestock.com; p. 30 Michele Damini/Shutterstock.com.

Cataloging-in-Publication Data

Names: Morrison, Marie.
Title: The Queen Mary is haunted! / Marie Morrison.
Description: New York : PowerKids Press, 2021. | Series: Haunted history | Includes glossary and index.
Identifiers: ISBN 9781725320000 (pbk.) | ISBN 9781725320024 (library bound) | ISBN 9781725320017 (6 pack)
Subjects: LCSH: Queen Mary (Steamship)--Juvenile literature. | Ghosts--Juvenile literature. | Haunted places --Juvenile literature.
Classification: LCC BF1486.M67 2021 | DDC 133.1'29--dc23

Manufactured in the United States of America

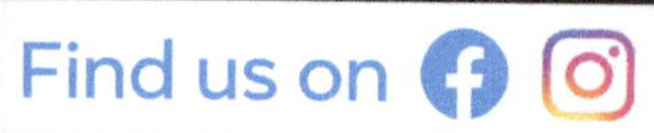

CONTENTS

A VERY UNUSUAL VESSEL

Do you believe in ghosts? Many people do, and many people don't. Still, people love to tell ghost stories, and some places tend to collect more of these stories than others. The ocean liner *Queen Mary* is one of these places. It's been a luxury ship transporting the rich and famous, a troopship carrying soldiers to the battlefields of World War II, and a floating hotel—a varied history that includes many chances for a stray spirit or two to linger on board.

The ship's long history includes many amazing tales, including some that are definitely real—and some that might not be. Still, the *Queen Mary* is a fascinating place with a creepy history. Read on and make up your own mind about whether it might be haunted!

THE *QUEEN MARY* CROSSED THE OCEAN 1,001 TIMES DURING ITS YEARS SAILING THE SEAS. THAT'S A LOT OF STORIES!

QUEEN MARY

THE STORY BEGINS

The *Queen Mary's* story started in 1930, when work began on what was then called "Job No. 534" in Scotland. Cunard Line, a British cruise line, meant the new ship to be a superliner, a bigger, faster **passenger** ship, to replace its existing ships. However, the **Great Depression** slowed the work, delaying it for years until construction resumed in 1934. That same year, the ship launched, leaving the docks for the rest of its work.

Finally, on May 27, 1936, the *Queen Mary* left England on its first voyage. It was the start of a new **era** in ocean liners. By the time the ship made its sixth voyage, the *Queen Mary* won the Blue Riband, an award for the fastest crossing of the North Atlantic Ocean.

SPOOKY STUFF

When the *Queen Mary* launched in 1934, a story says, a British **psychic** said, "The *Queen Mary* will know her greatest fame and popularity when she never sails another mile or carries another fare-paying passenger."

This picture, taken in 1911, shows King George V and his wife, Queen Mary. The ship was named after the queen.

STARS AT SEA

Because of its beauty, speed, and luxury, the *Queen Mary* drew many passengers who were rich, powerful, or famous—or all three! Hollywood stars including Clark Gable, Bob Hope, Fred Astaire, Elizabeth Taylor, Audrey Hepburn, and more crossed the ocean on the ship. So did powerful political leaders such as British Prime Minister Winston Churchill and General Dwight Eisenhower, who would later become the U.S. president.

All these passengers could take advantage of some of the most luxurious fittings of any ship of the time. The *Queen Mary* had five dining rooms, two swimming pools, a grand ballroom, beauty salons and barbershops, libraries, and a music studio. It was full of artwork and fine materials, including more than 50 types of wood from around the world.

SPOOKY STUFF

Much of the design of the Queen Mary was in the art deco style popular in the 1920s and 1930s. The art deco style uses new materials, strong outlines, and **geometric** shapes.

Actress Elizabeth Taylor, holding her pet poodles, is shown on the deck of the *Queen Mary* in 1947. The ship had dog kennels, too!

THE SHIP IN WARTIME

However, the *Queen Mary's* time in that type of spotlight was brief. In September 1939, England and France declared war on Germany, and World War II began. The ship's speed and size, points of pride during its days as a luxury liner, suddenly were entirely different advantages. By spring 1940, the Grey Ghost was born.

The *Queen Mary,* now painted grey and stripped of its many luxuries, began its time as a troopship, carrying soldiers to war across the sea. The ship carried as many as 16,683 people at a time, including leaders (such as Churchill), crew, soldiers, and sometimes prisoners of war. By 1946, the ship had carried more than 765,000 military personnel and sailed more than 569,000 miles (915,717 km).

SPOOKY STUFF

WINSTON CHURCHILL SECRETLY TRAVELED ON THE *QUEEN MARY* THREE TIMES DURING THE WAR. HE TRAVELED UNDER THE NAME "COLONEL WARDEN."

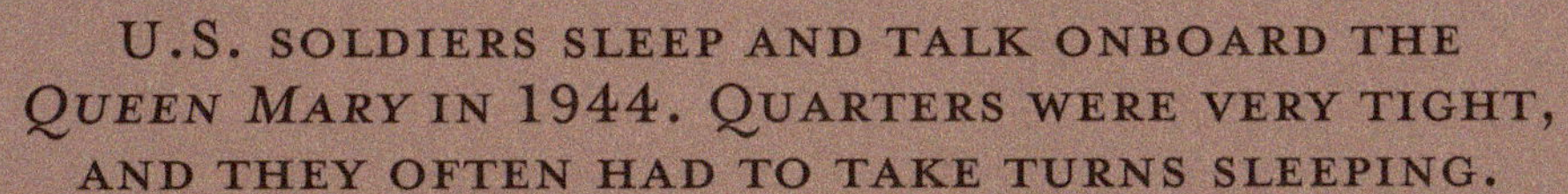

U.S. SOLDIERS SLEEP AND TALK ONBOARD THE *QUEEN MARY* IN 1944. QUARTERS WERE VERY TIGHT, AND THEY OFTEN HAD TO TAKE TURNS SLEEPING.

-A HAPPIER DUTY-

In 1946, after the war was over, the *Queen Mary* transported woman who'd married U.S. and Canadian soldiers from Europe to North America to join their husbands. The ship made these "war bride" voyages 13 times, carrying about 22,000 women and thousands of children to reunite with husbands and fathers. The WWII War Brides Association still has reunions on the ship today.

CHANGING TIMES

It took about 10 months to restore the *Queen Mary* to its status as a luxury ocean liner after the war. It set sail again on July 21, 1947, no longer the Grey Ghost. It was now joined by a new Cunard liner, the *Queen Elizabeth*. The *Queen Mary* continued to hold the Blue Riband for fastest Atlantic crossing until July 1952.

However, things were changing. By the 1950s, people could safely, comfortably, and quickly cross the ocean by airplane in hours instead of days on an ocean liner. In 1954, about 1 million people traveled across the Atlantic Ocean by ship, while about 600,000 traveled by plane. By 1965, about 650,000 traveled by ship and 4 million by plane. In 1966, Cunard announced that the *Queen Mary* was for sale.

THE *QUEEN MARY*, SHOWN IN 1952, HELD ITS SPEED RECORD UNTIL IT WAS SURPASSED BY THE SS *UNITED STATES* THAT YEAR. THE *UNITED STATES* RECORD STILL HOLDS FOR ANY SHIP OF ITS KIND.

QUEEN MARY

A FINAL VOYAGE

In 1967, the city of Long Beach in Southern California paid $3.45 million for the *Queen Mary.* The ship set sail for one last cruise on October 31, 1967, traveling from Great Britain to California with more than 1,000 passengers and about 800 crew members. It sailed down around South America and up the West Coast of North America.

On December 9, 1967, the *Queen Mary* arrived at its final home. It had carried more than 2.1 million passengers nearly 4 million miles (6.4 million km) over its time at sea. Once it arrived at Long Beach, however, workers renovated the ship and took out much of its seafaring equipment. The *Queen Mary* is now a ship permanently tied to the land.

SPOOKY STUFF

TODAY, THE *QUEEN MARY* IS A HOTEL, EVENTS CENTER, AND MUSEUM. VISITORS CAN STAY IN ITS 347 STATEROOMS AND **SUITES**, TAKE TOURS OF THE HISTORIC SHIP, AND EAT AT ITS RESTAURANTS.

More than 50 million people have stayed on the *Queen Mary* since it arrived at Long Beach. More than 12,000 people have been married there!

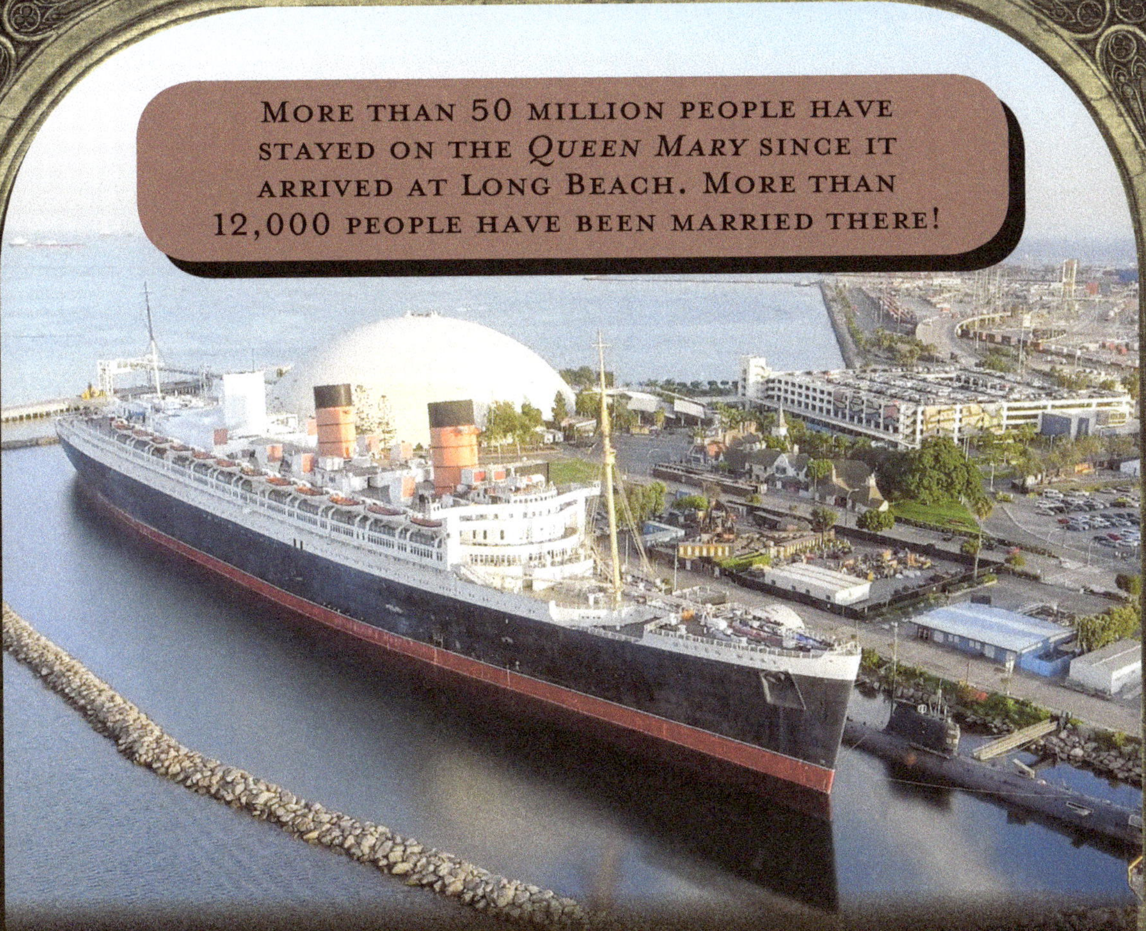

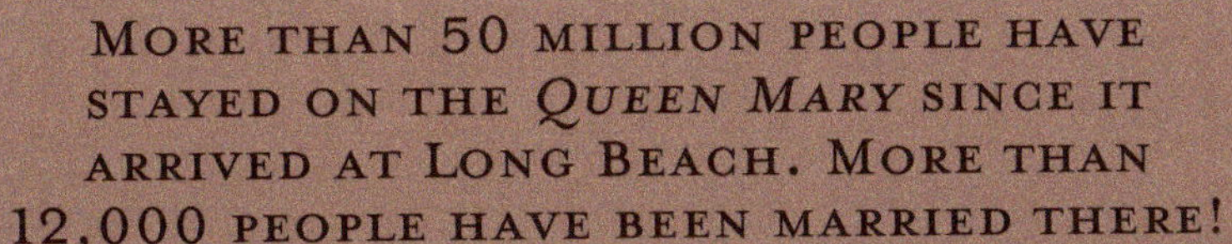

-Too Hot to Handle-

The *Queen Mary*, made to travel the Atlantic Ocean, wasn't built for the temperatures of the equator, which it crossed on its last voyage. All the ship's metal held in the heat. It was so hot that one of the ship's crewmen, a chef named Lock "Lobster" Horsborough, died of heat exhaustion and was buried at sea. Today, Horsborough's memory is preserved as one of the *Queen Mary's* many ghost stories. He's said to haunt the kitchen!

SPIRITS AND STORIES

With all its history and its varied roles, it's not much of a surprise that so many people think the *Queen Mary* is haunted. In fact, some call it one of the most haunted places in the world! Staff members and visitors have reported mysterious encounters and experiences on the ship.

These **phenomena** include temperature changes, strange sounds (such as knocks, cries, footsteps, phones ringing, and doors slamming), and even odd smells. And that's not even counting the **apparitions** reported: ghostly workers, children, men in suits, and women in white evening gowns. While only 49 deaths were reported on board the ship, stories tell of at least 150 spirits there. Is the *Queen Mary* really haunted? Read on, and decide for yourself!

TODAY, VISITORS CAN TAKE PART IN SEASONAL HAUNTED-HOUSE EVENTS AT THE *QUEEN MARY*. THIS PHOTO SHOWS SOME OF THE ACTORS.

MONSTER MIDWAY
AT
DARK HARBOR

DEAD POOLS

Both of the *Queen Mary's* swimming pools, while not used for guests today, seem to be popular with the hotel's more ghostly visitors. People have reported seeing women in 1930s-style swimsuits at the first-class pool, hearing splashing noises, and glimpsing wet footprints leading across the deck. However, there's no water in the pool—and there hasn't been for more than 30 years!

The second-class pool room is said to be home to one of the ship's most famous ghostly guests. Visitors say they've heard and seen a young girl there, **allegedly** the victim of a drowning back in the ship's luxury liner days. Some people even say they've recorded little "Jackie's" voice and communicated with her. Still, there's no record of any children or adults drowning on the ship.

SOME PEOPLE SAY JACKIE WILL LAUGH, HUM SONGS, OR CALL FOR HER PARENTS IN THE POOL ROOM, SHOWN HERE IN 1936.

-Haunted Playroom-

Sometimes people say they hear a baby crying in the third-class children's playroom on the ship. This is said to be the ghost of an infant who died on the ship, maybe the child of one of the war brides. (Some stories say its mother died as well.) Other times, visitors have seen a little girl holding a teddy bear or a young boy wearing blue.

THE CURACOA

One tragedy connected to the *Queen Mary* didn't kill anyone who was actually on the ship—but it did kill many other people. During World War II, the liner was so useful to the **Allies** that other ships would sometimes sail with it to protect it. On October 2, 1942, the HMS *Curacoa* was escorting the bigger ship.

Both ships were moving back and forth to confuse any German ships. Somehow (the stories vary), the much-larger liner struck the smaller *Curacoa* and sliced it right in half. More than 300 men died on the smaller ship and in the waters around it. Today, visitors on the *Queen Mary* sometimes report hearing the noise of crumpling metal and men screaming when they walk near the ship's lower **bow**.

THE *QUEEN MARY* WAS SO BIG THAT PEOPLE ON BOARD IT DURING THE TIME OF THE *CURACOA* CRASH SAID THEY ONLY FELT A BUMP.

-Left Behind-

The crew members of the *Queen Mary*—which was carrying thousands of soldiers—were under orders not to stop for any reason. The bigger ship (only slightly damaged) kept going after hitting the *Curacoa*, although the captain did signal other ships to pick up survivors. The water was so cold, however, that many men died of **hypothermia** before the other ships could arrive. About 100 men from the *Curacoa*, out of more than 430, survived.

SPOOKY SUITE

If you believe the stories, one of the creepiest places on the *Queen Mary* is stateroom B340. This space used to be three third-class rooms during the ship's days at sea. One tale says that a male passenger named Walter Adamson died in one of the rooms in 1948. Years later, a woman staying in the room reported that something pulled the covers off her while she slept—and that when she looked up, she saw a dark figure standing at the foot of the bed! However, it vanished when she screamed.

Hotel employees have also said the room's lights and sink faucet turn on and off by themselves. Guests report hearing odd knocks on the doors. Sometimes, the toilets flush with no one around.

In this photo, a *Queen Mary* tour guide stands in B340 in 2013. For a while, the room wasn't used because of the reports of ghostly activity.

-B340-

Suite B340 isn't as nice as some of the *Queen Mary's* other rooms, though it is big. Third-class rooms didn't have as many luxuries as first- and second-class rooms. This—and all the ghostly goings-on—don't seem to chase anyone off, though. In fact, today, tourists can pay nearly $499 a night to stay in this spooky suite. They even get ghost-hunting equipment to use.

THE UNLUCKY DOOR

The *Queen Mary's* engine room lies deep below water level on the ship. The doors there were watertight in case of an accident, and sometimes, the ship's crew would have emergency drills there. That much is definitely true.

It's also true that, during a drill early on July 10, 1966, an 18-year-old crew member named John Pedder died when he didn't make it through the heavy door marked "13" in time. He might have been playing a dangerous game, or he might have just been trying to squeeze through the doorway a little late. Either way, the door crushed him as it closed.

That's where the ghost stories come in, of course. Pedder is now said to haunt "Shaft Alley," the hallway from the engine room to the back of the ship.

SPOOKY STUFF

FILMMAKERS USED THE *QUEEN MARY'S* ENGINE ROOM AND DOOR 13 IN THE 1972 MOVIE *THE POSEIDON ADVENTURE*.

The engine room doors closed automatically during drills or emergencies. Crew members had 60 seconds to get through.

GRUMPY, GROWLING GHOST

Another of the *Queen Mary's* most well-known ghost guests is the apparition known as Grumpy. Stories say he growls at startled visitors and tends to hang out under the stairs near the first-class pool room or in the boiler room. Sometimes, the smell of cigarette smoke drifts after him. Some people say they've seen glowing eyes looking out at them from his spot under the stairs!

There are other named ghosts on the ship. Young sailor John Henry also allegedly haunts the boiler room, where he once supposedly worked. The ghost named Sarah is said to hang out with little Jackie in the pool room and other locations—though she's said to be a little more mischievous, even pushing or slapping people.

Sometimes, John Henry is said to haunt the engine room, shown here during a tour in 2014.

DEADLY ERROR

One of the *Queen Mary's* rumored ghosts may be truly embarrassed about how he got there. Naval officer William E. Stark, the stories say, was working on the ship in September 1949. He was apparently looking for a clear kind of alcohol called gin to make drinks. However, what Stark (or maybe another worker, depending on the **version** of the story) found was something else altogether.

Instead of gin, Stark used a cleaning liquid called tetrachloride to make a drink. When he found out about his mistake, he reportedly laughed about it and refused to have his stomach cleaned out. He died a few days later of poisoning. Some people say his ghost, still in his uniform, continues to walk the ship's decks today.

Stories say Stark can sometimes be seen or heard on the ship's decks or in the captain's cabin.

THE TALES CONTINUE

Today, Long Beach and those who run the *Queen Mary* as a hotel take advantage of its spooky reputation. There are tours and packages to show off the "most haunted" sites on board and special Halloween events. Visitors can rent and stay in Room B340. Ghost hunters stop by to film, record, and investigate the hallways and rooms.

Whether or not you believe in ghosts, it can be fun to listen to the stories and imagine the possibilities. The *Queen Mary* has a long and interesting history, from its origins as a luxury ship though its years at war and its present as a hotel. There are countless stories that have to do with its many passengers over the decades. Who knows? Maybe some of those passengers are still there!

GLOSSARY

allegedly: Said to have happened but not proven.

Allies: The group of nations, including England and the United States, in World War II that opposed the Axis nations, including Germany and Japan.

apparition: A ghost or spirit.

bow: The front of a boat or ship.

era: A period of time associated with something in particular.

geometric: Having to do with straight lines, circles, and other simple shapes.

Great Depression: A period of economic struggle in the United States and much of the world from 1929 to 1939.

hypothermia: Dangerously low body temperature caused by cold conditions.

passenger: Someone who rides on a plane, car, boat, ship, or bus.

phenomenon: A fact or event that is observed.

psychic: Relating to supernatural abilities, energy, or knowledge.

suite: A group of rooms used for one purpose.

version: A form of something that is different from the ones that came before it.

INDEX

WEBSITES

Due to the changing nature of Internet links, PowerKids Press has developed an online list of websites related to the subject of this book. This site is updated regularly. Please use this link to access the list: www.powerkidslinks.com/haunted/queenmary